THE EMPEROR'S NEW CLOTHES

AND OTHER STORIES

HANS CHRISTIAN ANDERSEN

THE EMPEROR'S NEW CLOTHES

AND OTHER STORIES

Translated by
Erik Christian Haugaard

penguin books

PENGUIN BOOKS
Published by the Penguin Group
Penguin Books USA Inc., 375 Hudson Street,
New York, New York 10014, U.S.A.
Penguin Books Ltd, 27 Wrights Lane, London W8 5TZ, England
Penguin Books Australia Ltd, Ringwood, Victoria, Australia
Penguin Books Canada Ltd, 10 Alcorn Avenue,
Toronto, Ontario, Canada M4V 3B2
Penguin Books (N.Z.) Ltd, 182–190 Wairau Road,
Auckland 10, New Zealand

Penguin Books Ltd, Registered Offices:
Harmondsworth, Middlesex, England

These stories are taken from *The Penguin Complete Fairy Tales and Stories of Hans Andersen*, published by Penguin Books.
This edition published 1995.

ISBN 0 14 60.0030 7

Printed in the United States of America

CONTENTS

The Emperor's New Clothes

Many, many years ago there was an emperor who was so terribly fond of beautiful new clothes that he spent all his money on his attire. He did not care about his soldiers, or attending the theatre, or even going for a drive in the park, unless it was to show off his new clothes. He had an outfit for every hour of the day. And just as we say, 'The king is in his council chamber,' his subjects used to say, 'The emperor is in his clothes closet.'

In the large town where the emperor's palace was, life was gay and happy; and every day new visitors arrived. One day two swindlers came. They told everybody that they were weavers and that they could weave the most marvellous cloth. Not only were the colours and the patterns of their material extraordinarily beautiful, but the cloth had the strange quality of being invisible to anyone who was unfit for his office, or unforgivably stupid.

'This is truly marvellous,' thought the emperor. 'Now if I had robes cut from that material, I should know which of my councillors was unfit for his office, and I would be able to pick out my clever subjects myself. They must weave some material for me!' And he gave the swindlers a lot of money so they could start working at once.

They set up a loom and acted as if they were weaving, but the loom was empty. The fine silk and gold threads they demanded from the emperor they never used, but hid them in their own knapsacks. Late into the night they would sit before their empty loom, pretending to weave.

'I would like to know how they are getting along,' thought the emperor; but his heart beat strangely when he remembered that those who were stupid or unfit for their office would not be able to see the material. Not that he was really worried that this would happen to him. Still, it might be better to send someone else the first time and see how he fared. Everybody in town had heard about the cloth's magic quality and most of them could hardly wait to find out how stupid or unworthy their neighbours were.

'I shall send my faithful prime minister over to see how the weavers are getting along,' thought the emperor. 'He will know how to judge the material, for he is both clever and fit for his office, if any man is.'

The good-natured old man stepped into the room where the weavers were working and saw the empty loom. He closed his eyes, and opened them again. 'God preserve me!' he thought. 'I cannot see a thing!' But he didn't say it out loud.

The swindlers asked him to step a little closer to the

loom so that he could admire the intricate patterns and marvellous colours of the material they were weaving. They both pointed to the empty loom, and the poor old prime minister opened his eyes as wide as he could; but it didn't help, he still couldn't see anything.

'Am I stupid?' he thought. 'I can't believe it, but if it is so, it is best no one finds out about it. But maybe I am not fit for my office. No, that is worse, I'd better not admit that I can't see what they are weaving.'

'Tell us what you think of it,' demanded one of the swindlers.

'It is beautiful. It is lovely,' mumbled the old prime minister, adjusting his glasses. 'What patterns! What colours! I shall tell the emperor that it pleases me ever so much.'

'That is a compliment,' both the weavers said; and now they described the patterns and told which shades of colour they had used. The prime minister listened attentively, so that he could repeat their words to the emperor; and that is exactly what he did.

The two swindlers demanded more money, and more silk and gold thread. They said they had to use it for their weaving, but their loom remained as empty as ever.

Soon the emperor sent another of his trusted councillors to see how the work was progressing. He looked and looked just as the prime minister had, but since there was nothing to be seen, he didn't see anything.

'Isn't it a marvellous piece of material?' asked one of the swindlers; and they both began to describe the beauty of their cloth again.

'I am not stupid,' thought the emperor's councillor. 'I must be unfit for my office. That is strange; but I'd better not admit it to anyone.' And he started to praise the material, which he could not see, for the loveliness of its patterns and colours.

'I think it is the most charming piece of material I have ever seen,' declared the councillor to the emperor.

Everyone in town was talking about the marvellous cloth that the swindlers were weaving.

At last the emperor himself decided to see it before it was removed from the loom. Attended by the most important people in the empire, among them the prime minister and the councillor who had been there before, the emperor entered the room where the weavers were weaving furiously on their empty loom.

'Isn't it *magnifique*?' asked the prime minister.

'Your Majesty, look at the colours and the patterns,' said the councillor.

And the two old gentlemen pointed to the empty loom, believing that all the rest of the company could see the cloth.

'What!' thought the emperor. 'I can't see a thing! Why, this is a disaster! Am I stupid? Am I unfit to be emperor? Oh, it is too horrible!' Aloud, he said, 'It is very lovely. It has my approval,' while he nodded his head and looked at the empty loom.

All the councillors, ministers, and men of great importance who had come with him stared, and stared; but they saw no more than the emperor had seen, and they said the same thing that he had said, 'It is lovely.' And they advised him to have clothes cut and sewn, so that he could wear them in the procession at the next great celebration.

'It is magnificent! Beautiful! Excellent!' All of their mouths agreed, though none of their eyes had seen anything. The two swindlers were decorated and given the title 'Royal Knight of the Loom'.

The night before the procession, the two swindlers didn't sleep at all. They had sixteen candles lighting up the room where they worked. Everyone could see how busy they were, getting the emperor's new clothes finished. They pretended to take the cloth from the loom; they cut the air with their big scissors, and sewed with needles without thread. At last they announced: 'The emperor's clothes are ready!'

Together with his courtiers, the emperor came. The swindlers lifted their arms as if they were holding something in their hands, and said, 'These are the trousers.

This is the robe, and there is the train. They are all as light as if they were made of spider webs! It will be as if Your Majesty had almost nothing on, but that is their special virtue.'

'Oh yes,' breathed all the courtiers; but they saw nothing, for there was nothing to be seen.

'Will Your Imperial Majesty be so gracious as to take off your clothes?' asked the swindlers. 'Over there by the big mirror, we shall help you put your new ones on.'

The emperor did as he was told; and the swindlers acted as if they were dressing him in the clothes they should have made. Finally they tied around his waist the long train which two of his most noble courtiers were to carry.

The emperor stood in front of the mirror admiring the clothes he couldn't see.

'Oh, how they suit you! A perfect fit!' everyone exclaimed. 'What colours! What patterns! The new clothes are magnificent!'

'The crimson canopy, under which Your Imperial Majesty is to walk, is waiting outside,' said the imperial master of court ceremony.

'Well, I am dressed. Aren't my clothes becoming?' The emperor turned around once more in front of the mirror, pretending to study his finery.

 The two gentlemen of the imperial bedchamber fumbled

on the floor, trying to find the train which they were supposed to carry. They didn't dare admit that they didn't see anything, so they pretended to pick up the train and held their hands as if they were carrying it.

The emperor walked in the procession under his crimson canopy. And all the people of the town, who had lined the streets or were looking down from the windows, said that the emperor's clothes were beautiful. 'What a magnificent robe! And the train! How well the emperor's clothes suit him!'

None of them were willing to admit that they hadn't seen a thing; for if anyone did, then he was either stupid or unfit for the job he held. Never before had the emperor's clothes been such a success.

'But he doesn't have anything on!' cried a little child.

'Listen to the innocent one,' said the proud father. And the people whispered among each other and repeated what the child had said.

'He doesn't have anything on. There's a little child who says that he has nothing on.'

'He has nothing on!' shouted all the people at last.

The emperor shivered, for he was certain that they were right; but thought, 'I must bear it until the procession is over.' And he walked even more proudly, and the two gentlemen of the imperial bedchamber went on carrying the train that wasn't there.

The Bronze Pig

In the town of Florence, not far from the Piazza del Granduca, there is a little street – I believe that it is called Porta Rossa – and there across from a small market place, where vegetables are sold, stands a fountain cast in the shape of a pig. Clear, fresh water spouts from its snout, which shines as brightly as bronze can, while the rest of the body is green with age. The snout is polished daily by schoolboys and beggars who rest their hands upon it, while leaning over to drink. It is a lovely sight to see the beautifully made animal embraced by a thirsty half-naked boy, who almost kisses its ancient snout with his fresh, young mouth.

Anyone who visits Florence can find the fountain; and if he can't, he need only ask the first beggar he meets, and he will show him the way to the bronze pig.

It was late on a winter evening. The tops of the hills that surround the city were covered with snow. But it was not dark, for the moon was out; and the moon in Italy gives as much light as the sun does on a northern winter day. – No, I would even say that it gives more, for here the air is so clear, it seems to reflect the moon's light; it is not cold and grey as the air in the north, which like a leaden lid seems to be pressing you down into the cold, wet earth, as if you were already buried and lying in your coffin.

In the ducal gardens, where thousands of flowers bloom in winter, a ragged little boy had sat all day under a large pine tree. He was the very picture of Italy: laughing, beautiful, and suffering. He was hungry and thirsty; and though he had held out his little hand all day no one had dropped anything into it. Night fell, and the watchman who came to close the gardens drove him away. On a bridge over the Arno, the boy stood for a long time, staring into the water and dreaming, as he watched the reflections of the many stars, the beautiful marble bridge called Santa Trinità, and himself, shimmering in the river.

He walked back to the fountain, and, putting his arms around the bronze pig's neck, he drank water from its shining spout. Nearby he found some lettuce leaves and a few chestnuts, and they were his dinner. It was cold and the streets were deserted. He was alone. He climbed up on the pig's back and, leaning his curly head forward so that it rested on the pig's head, he fell asleep.

It was midnight. The metal animal beneath him moved and said very distinctly, 'Little boy, hold on tight, for I am going to run!'

And it did run; and thus began the strangest ride that

anyone has ever taken. The pig went first to the Piazza del Granduca. The bronze horse, on which the duke was mounted, neighed loudly when it saw them. All the coloured coats of arms of the old town hall shone brilliantly; Michelangelo's David swung his sling. Every statue was alive. The metal figures around Perseus were much too alive; and the Sabine women screamed that horrible cry of fear before death, and it echoed throughout the beautiful square.

In the arcade of the Palazzo degli Uffizi, where the nobles of Florence gathered for their masquerades, the bronze pig stopped.

'Hold tight,' the bronze pig warned, 'for now we are going up the stairs.' The little boy did not answer; half joyfully, half fearfully, he clutched the neck of the pig.

They entered the long gallery. The boy knew it well, he had been there before: the walls were covered with paintings and here were the loveliest statues. But now the gallery was more brilliantly lighted than during the day; and every painting seemed more colourful, every bust and figure more beautiful. But the most magnificent moment – and that one the boy never would forget – was when the door to one of the smaller rooms opened. Here was the sculpture of a naked woman: beauty as only nature, marble, and the greatest of all artists can create it. She moved her lovely limbs, and the dolphins at her feet arched their backs and leaped about. Immortality was the message that could be read in her eyes. This sculpture is known to the world as the Medici Venus. On either side of her stood a marble statue, each proving that man's spirit and art can give life, can create it from lifeless stone. One of the figures was of a man grinding his sword; the other showed two gladiators wrestling: for beauty's sake the weapon was sharpened and the men fought.

The boy was almost blinded by the radiance of the colours of paintings on the walls. There was Titian's Venus, the mortal woman whom the artist had loved, stretching herself out on her soft couch. She tossed her head, her naked breasts heaved; her curly hair fell on her naked shoulders, and her dark eyes revealed the passion of the blood that flowed in her veins.

Although every work of art was intensely alive, they did not dare to leave their frames or their pedestals. Maybe it was the golden halos of the Madonna, Jesus, and John the Baptist that made them all stay in their places, for the holy paintings were no longer works of art, they were the holy person they portrayed.

What beauty! What loveliness! The little boy saw it all, for the bronze pig walked slowly through every room of the palace.

One magnificent work of art superseded the other. But one painting appealed especially to the boy, because there were children in it. He had seen it once before in the daylight. It was the painting of *Jesus Descending into the Underworld;* and many hasten by it without a glance, not realizing that it contains a whole world of poetry. The painter, a Florentine, Agnolo Bronzino, had not chosen to portray the suffering of the dead but the expectation in their faces at the sight of Our Lord. Two of the children are embracing; one little boy stretches his hand out towards another child, at the same time he points to himself, as if he were saying: 'I am going to Paradise.' Some of the older people in the painting look uncertain. Filled as they are with doubt and hope, they beg humbly, while the children, in their innocence, demand.

The boy looked at that painting longer than he did at any of the others, and the bronze pig patiently stood still in front of it.

Someone sighed. Did the sound come from the painting or the bronze pig? The boy lifted his hands toward the children in the painting; but just at that moment the pig turned and ran through the galleries.

'Thank you and God bless you!' whispered the boy as the pig went bumpity . . . bumpity . . . down the stairs with him on his back.

'Thank yourself and God bless you!' replied the metal animal. 'I have helped you and you have helped me, for only when an innocent child sits on my back, do I become alive and have the strength to run as I have tonight. Yes, I can even let the light from the lamp beneath the Blessed Virgin shine upon me. It is only into the church that I am not allowed to go; but with you on my back I can peep through the door. But don't try to get down, for if you do, then I shall be dead as I am in the daylight, when you see me in the Via Porta Rossa.'

'I will stay with you,' the child promised; and away they ran, through the streets of the town, till they came to the Church of Santa Croce.

The portals of the church opened by themselves. All the candles on the great altar were lit, and the light shone all the way out to the deserted square, where stood the bronze pig with a boy mounted on his back.

Above a tomb, along the left aisle, a thousand stars formed a halo. A coat of arms decorated the simple monument: on a blue background was a ladder that glowed as if it were on fire. It was the tomb of Galileo and the coat of arms could be the emblem of art itself, for the way of the artist is up a ladder of fire to the sky. Every true prophet of the spirit ascends towards heaven like Elijah!

Down the right aisle, all the marble figures on the richly decorated sarcophagi had come alive. Dante with laurel leaves on his head, Michelangelo, Machiavelli, Alfieri: here they were, side by side, the glory of Italy! The

Church of Santa Croce is not as large as Florence's cathedral, but it is much more beautiful.

The marble clothes of the statues seemed to move, while the great men's heads appeared to have turned so that they could look out into the night. From the altar came the sweet voices of the white-clad choir boys, who swung censers, from which the strong smell of incense pervaded the air, even as far as the square.

The boy stretched his arms towards the light of the altar, and the bronze pig turned and ran so fast that the child had to hold on with all his strength not to fall off. The boy heard the wind whistling in his ears, then he heard a loud bang as the big doors of the church closed. He lost consciousness. He felt cold; then he opened his eyes, he was awake.

It was morning. He was sitting – almost falling off – the bronze pig, which stood as immobile as ever in the Via Porta Rossa.

Fearfully, the boy thought of the woman whom he called his mother. She had sent him but yesterday to beg, but no one had given him any money, not so much as the tiniest copper coin. He was hungry. Once more he embraced the bronze pig and drank water from its snout. He kissed it and made his way home through the dirty streets.

He lived in one of the narrowest lanes in the city; it was just broad enough for a loaded donkey to pass. An iron-studded door stood ajar; he slipped past it and began to climb a stone staircase that had a worn-out rope for a banister. The walls were filthy. He came to the courtyard; above there was a gallery all the way around the building. On its railings, clothes that were no more than rags had been hung out to dry. In the centre of the yard there was a well, and from it heavy wires were strung to each of the apartments, so that water could be drawn without the inconvenience of having to carry it from below; and the pails danced in the air, spilling water down into the courtyard.

The boy went up another, even narrower, stone staircase. Two Russian sailors who were coming from their night's bacchanal were rushing down the stairs, laughing, and they almost bumped into the child. A woman who was neither young nor old, with beautiful black hair, stood on the landing at the top of the stairs.

'How much did you get?' she asked the boy.

'Don't be angry!' he begged. 'I didn't get anything; nothing at all!' The boy grabbed the hem of her skirt as if he were, in humility, about to kiss it.

They stepped inside, into the garret that was their home. Its misery I shall not describe. Only one thing needs to be mentioned: there was an earthenware pot filled with smouldering charcoal, and the woman put her hands around it in order to warm them.

She poked the child with her elbow and screamed, 'Where is the money? I know you have money!'

The boy started to weep. She kicked out at him with her foot, and he wailed louder. 'Keep still, you snivelling little thing, or I'll bash your head in!' She swung the earthenware pot in the air as if she were about to carry out her threat. Screaming, the child threw himself down on the floor.

Another woman came rushing into the room. She, too, was carrying a dish containing burning charcoal. 'Felicita, what are you doing to the child?' she said.

'He's my child, and I can murder him if I want to,' the woman answered. 'And I can kill you too, Gianina!' And she flung her clay pot towards the intruder; and Gianina lifted hers in order to ward off the danger; and the two dishes met in mid-air, breaking in pieces and spreading burning charcoal all over the tiny room.

But the child had escaped. He ran down the stairs, across the courtyard, and out of the house. He ran as fast as he could, and he kept on running until he could hardly breathe. He had reached the Church of Santa Croce. He entered the church whose portals had opened for him the night before and he kneeled down in front of one of the tombs; it was Michelangelo's. Still crying, he prayed. The only one, among all those who had come to attend mass, to notice him was an elderly man. He glanced at the child and then walked on.

The little boy felt weak from hunger. He climbed into the niche between the monument and the wall and fell asleep. He was awakened by someone tugging at his sleeve. It was the man who had been in the church earlier in the day.

'Are you ill?' the man demanded. 'Where do you live?' He went on asking questions. The boy answered him; and finally the man took him by the hand and led him to his home.

It was a small house in one of the side streets. The man was a glovemaker and his wife was sitting sewing gloves when they entered. A little white poodle, whose curly coat was cut so closely that its pink skin could be seen, hopped up on a table and sprang up on the boy, barking all the while.

'The two innocent souls recognize each other,' said the woman, and patted the dog.

The boy was given something to eat and allowed to stay for the night. The next day the glovemaker, Papa Giuseppi as he was called, would talk with his mother. The boy was given a bed to sleep on which was no more than a bench; but to the child who was used to sleeping on a stone floor, it seemed royal luxury. That night he dreamed about the bronze pig and the paintings he had seen.

When Papa Giuseppi left the house the next morning, the little boy was not happy. He was afraid that he would be taken back to his mother, and he cried and kissed the little dog. The glovemaker's wife smiled and nodded to them both.

When Papa Giuseppi came home, he talked with his wife for a long time alone. When they were finished, she patted the child on the head and said kindly, 'He is a sweet little boy. He can be as good a glovemaker as you are. Look at his fingers, how long and thin they are. I am sure Our Lady has meant for him to be a glovemaker.'

The boy stayed in their home and the glovemaker's wife taught him how to sew. He was given plenty to eat, and he slept comfortably in his little bed. Soon his boyish spirit returned and he began to tease Bellissima, the little dog. This the glovemaker's wife did not like. She was angry; she shook her finger at him and scolded him.

The child was sorry for what he had done. Thoughtful and repentant, he sat in his tiny room, which was also used for drying skins. There were bars on the window, to prevent thieves from entering it. That night he could not sleep. Suddenly he heard a noise outside the window. *Clappidy . . . Clap . . .* The boy felt certain that it was the bronze pig who had come to comfort him. He jumped out of bed and ran to the window. He saw only the empty alley.

'Help the *signore* to carry his paints,' the woman said to the boy the following morning. The *signore* was their neighbour, a young painter. He was having difficulty carrying both a large canvas and his box of paints.

The boy took the paint box, and together they went to the gallery: the same one the boy had visited with the bronze pig. The child recognized many of the beautiful marble statues and the paintings. There was the lovely statue of Venus; and he saw again the pictures of Jesus, the Holy Mother, and John the Baptist.

The painter stopped in front of the painting of *Jesus Descending into the Underworld* by Bronzino, in which the children smile so sweetly in their certainty that soon they will be in Heaven. The little boy smiled too, for this was his Heaven.

'Now you can go home,' said the painter, when he noticed that the boy was still there, after he finished setting up his easel.

'May I not watch you paint, sir?' the boy asked as courteously as he could. 'I would so like to know how it is done.'

'I am not going to paint now, I am only going to draw,' explained the artist. In his hand he had a black crayon; how swiftly it moved across the white surface! With his eye he measured the figures in the painting, and soon the outline of Christ appeared.

'Don't stand there gaping. Go home,' ordered the painter irritably.

The boy wandered back to the house of the glover, sat down at the table, and started to sew gloves. But his mind was still on the paintings he had seen, and he pricked his fingers and sewed badly, that day. But he did not tease Bellissima.

That evening he noticed that the street door was open and he tiptoed outside. It was a chilly but beautiful starry night. Slowly he walked toward the Via Porta Rossa to see the bronze pig.

He bent down, kissed the pig on its shiny snout, and then mounted its back. 'Blessed animal,' he whispered in its ear, 'I have longed for you. Tonight we shall ride again.'

But the bronze pig was motionless, the clear, fresh water flowing from its mouth. Suddenly the boy felt something tugging at his trouser leg. It was Bellissima, the naked little dog – even in this light he could see its pink skin beneath its short cropped hair. The dog barked, as if it were saying, 'Look, I have followed you. Why are you sitting up there?'

A goblin could not have frightened the boy more than the dog did. Bellissima out in the street at night, without her little sheepskin coat on! The dog was never allowed out in the winter without the coat that had been made especially for her. It was tied at the neck with a red ribbon, and it had little belts that were buckled under its stomach. The little dog looked like a little lamb when it went out walking with its mistress, the glovemaker's wife. How the boy feared her anger when she found out that her darling was not at home!

His wish to ride again with the bronze pig was gone, though he kissed the metal animal as he slid off its back. He picked up the dog which was so cold, it was shivering. And the boy ran, with Bellissima in his arms, as fast as he could toward the glover's house.

'Where are running?' shouted a policeman. Bellissima began to bark. 'Have you stolen this dog?' demanded the policeman, taking the animal from him.

'Oh, give it back to me!' wailed the boy.

'If it's really yours – and you haven't stolen it – then you can tell them at home that they can get it back by coming to the police station.' And the policeman told the frightened child on which street the police station was to be found, and walked away with Bellissima in his arms.

How miserable the poor little boy was! He didn't know whether he should go to the glovemaker's and tell what had happened, or jump in the Arno. 'She will kill me,' he thought. 'But I don't mind dying for them. I will go up to heaven to the Blessed Virgin and Jesus.' Having made his decision, he walked home to tell all and be killed.

The door was locked and he could not reach the

knocker. The street was empty. He found a stone and banged on the door with it.

'Who's there?' shouted a voice from inside.

'It's me!' screamed the little boy. 'Bellissima is gone! Open up the door and kill me!'

They were shocked, especially the glovemaker's wife. Her glance went at once to the peg where the little dog's sheepskin coat was still hanging.

'Bellissima at the police station!' she screamed. 'You evil child! How could you have taken her out in such cold weather? The poor dog will freeze to death! That little gentle creature in the hands of such ruffians as the police!'

The glovemaker rushed out of the house to go to the police station and retrieve the dog. His wife kept on screaming, and the boy kept on crying. They made such a lot of noise that all the people in the house were awakened and came down to see what was happening, including the painter.

The artist took the boy on his lap; and slowly the child told him the whole story of the bronze pig and his visit to the Galleria degli Uffizi. The painter shook his head in wonder; it was a strange story. He comforted the boy and tried to calm the glovemaker's wife, but it was impossible. Not until her husband had returned with the little dog did she stop lamenting and wailing. Though when she had examined Bellissima and realized that she didn't seem any the worse for having associated with the police, she did cheer up.

The painter patted the boy on the head and gave him some drawings as a gift. They were marvellous drawings! Some of them were caricatures and very funny, but the picture that the boy loved most was the one of the bronze pig. Only a few lines on a piece of paper and there it was, and even the house behind the fountain was there too.

'If you can draw and paint,' thought the child, 'then you can call the whole world your own.'

The next day, as soon as he had finished his work he took a pencil stub and tried to copy the sketch of the bronze pig on the back of one of the artist's drawings. He succeeded! Well, he almost did – one of the legs was a little too long and another was too thin; but still, the pig was there on paper. Joyfully, the boy tried again the following day. It was not easy to make the pencil draw lines as straight as he wanted them to be. But the second pig was better than the first; and the third one, anyone could have recognized.

Although his drawing improved, his glove-sewing did not, and when he was sent on errands it took him longer and longer to return, for the bronze pig had taught him that all pictures can be drawn; and Florence is one enormous picture book, for anyone who cares to turn the pages. On the Piazza Santa Trinità there stands a slender column with a statue of Justice on top of it; the goddess is blindfolded and has a pair of scales in her hands. Soon he not only stood on a column, but also on a sheet of paper, for the boy had drawn her.

The folio of the glovemaker's little apprentice was growing; but until now he had only drawn dead, immobile objects. One day Bellissima was romping gaily about him.

'Sit still,' he said to the dog, 'and I shall make a lovely picture of you for my collection.'

But Bellissima would neither sit nor stand still. If the boy wanted to draw it, there was nothing else for him to do but tie the animal. The child tied the dog both by the tail and by the neck, which the animal didn't like in the least. It barked and tried to jump; and at last the *signora* came.

'You unchristian boy!' she cried. 'Oh, the poor animal!' And she kicked the child. 'You ungrateful wretch!' she screamed while she picked up the half-strangled little dog and kissed it. Then she dragged the weeping child out of her home.

At that very moment the painter came down the stairs; and this is the turning point of the story.

In Florence, in 1834, there was an exhibition at the Academy of Art. Two paintings that hung next to each other attracted special attention. The smaller one portrayed a little boy who was sketching a closely cropped little white poodle; the dog had not wanted to stand still and the artist had tethered it with strings around both her neck and her tail. The painting was strangely alive, and there was a loveliness about it that revealed the artist's talent. It was told that the painter was born in Florence and had been found in the streets by an elderly glovemaker who had taken the child in. He had taught himself how to draw. A famous painter had discovered the boy's ability, on the very day that the glover's wife had thrown him out of her house for having tied up her darling poodle, so that he could use him as a model.

The glovemaker's little apprentice had become a great artist; this was proven by the other painting as well. It was a picture of a boy, so poor that his clothes were rags, sleeping on the back of the bronze pig in the Via Porta Rossa. Everyone who saw the painting knew the street and the fountain. The child's arm was resting on the pig's head. The little lamp on the wall under the image of the Blessed Virgin cast its light on the child's pale, beautiful face. It was a marvellous painting, framed in gold. On the very top of the frame was a laurel wreath; among the green leaves there was a band of black crepe, and a long black ribbon hung down the side of the painting.

Only a few days before, the young painter had died!

Little Claus and Big Claus

Once upon a time there lived in a village two men who had the same name; they were both called Claus. But one of them owned four horses, while the other had only one; so to tell them apart the richer man was called Big Claus and the poorer one Little Claus. Now let's hear what happened to the two of them because that's a real story!

Six days a week Little Claus had to work for Big Claus and lend him his horse; and in return Big Claus had to let Little Claus borrow his four horses on Sunday. One day a week Little Claus felt as if all the horses belonged to him, and he would crack his whip in the air and shout orders to them merrily.

One morning when the sun was shining brightly and the villagers, all dressed up in their Sunday best, with their prayer books under their arms, were passing his field, Little Claus cracked his whip in the air, whistled, and called out very loudly, 'Gee up, all my horses!'

'You may not say that!' exclaimed Big Claus. 'Only one of the horses is yours.'

But Little Claus forgot very quickly what Big Claus had said, and the next time someone went by and nodded kindly in his direction, he shouted, 'Gee up, all my horses!'

Big Claus turned around and shouted! 'I beg you for the last time not to call all those horses yours because if you do it once more, I'll take the mallet that I use to drive in the stake for tethering my four horses and hit your one horse so hard that it will drop dead on the spot.'

'I promise never to say it again,' said Little Claus meekly. But the words were hardly out of his mouth when still another group of churchgoers stopped to watch him plough. They smiled and said good morning in a very friendly way. 'What a fine figure I must cut, driving five horses,' he thought; and without realizing what he was doing, he cracked the whip and cried, 'Gee up, all my horses!'

'I'll give your horse gee up!' screamed Big Claus in a rage; and he took his tethering mallet and hit Little Claus's only horse so hard on the forehead that it fell down quite dead.

'Poor me!' cried Little Claus. 'Now I haven't got a horse at all!' And he sat down and wept. But as there was nothing else to do he flayed the horse and hung the hide up to dry. When the wind had done its work, Little Claus put the hide in a sack and set off for town to sell it in the market place.

It was a long way and the road led through a forest.

The weather turned bad and among the dark shadows Little Claus lost his way. He turned first in one direction and then in another. Finally he did find his way again; but by then it was late afternoon and too late to reach town before nightfall.

Not far from the road he saw a farmhouse. The shutters were closed but above them there shone tiny streams of light. 'There I may ask for shelter for the night,' Little Claus thought, and made his way to the front door and knocked.

The farmer's wife answered the door, but when she heard what be wanted she shook her head. 'You'll have to go away,' she ordered. 'My husband isn't home and I cannot allow a stranger to come in.'

'Then I'll have to sleep outside,' said Little Claus. The farmer's wife shut the door without another word; and Little Claus looked about him. Near the house was a haystack, and between that and the dwelling there was a shed with a flat thatched roof.

'I'll stretch out on that,' Little Claus mumbled, looking at the roof. 'It will make a fine bed and I doubt if the stork will fly down and bite me.' The latter was said in jest because there was a stork's nest on the roof of the farmhouse.

Little Claus climbed up on the roof of the shack; and
 while he was twisting and turning to make himself comfort-

able, he realized that from where he lay he could see right into the kitchen of the farmhouse because, at the top, the shutters did not close tightly.

A fine white linen cloth covered the large table and on it were not only a roast and wine but a platter of fish as well. On one side of the table sat the farmer's wife and on the other the deacon; and while she filled his glass with wine, he filled himself with fish because that was his favourite food.

'If only I had been invited too!' Little Claus sighed, and pushed himself as near to the window as he could without touching the shutters. There was a cake on the table too; this was better than a party, it was a feast!

He heard someone galloping on the road; he turned and saw the rider: it was the farmer coming home.

Now this farmer was known for two things: one, that he was a good fellow, and the other, that he suffered from a strange disease; he couldn't bear the sight of a deacon. One glance and he went into a rage. And that, of course, was the reason why the deacon had come visiting on a day when the farmer wasn't at home; and that too was why the farmer's wife had made the most delicious food she could for her guest.

When they heard the farmer riding up to the door of his house, both the farmer's wife and the deacon were terrified; and she told him to climb into a large empty chest that stood in the corner. The poor man, trembling with fear, obeyed her. Then the woman hid all the food and the wine in the oven, for she knew that if her husband saw all the delicacies he was certain to ask her why she had made them.

'Ow!' groaned Little Claus when he saw the last of the food disappear into the bread oven.

'Is there someone up there?' the farmer called, and when he saw Little Claus lying on the roof of the shed he told him to come down. 'What were you doing up there?'

Little Claus explained how he had lost his way in the forest and asked the farmer to be allowed to spend the night in his house.

'You are most welcome,' said the farmer, who was the kindest of men, as long as there was no deacon in sight. 'But first let's have a bite to eat.'

The farmer's wife greeted them both very politely, set the table, and served them a large bowl of porridge. The farmer, who was very hungry, ate with relish; but Little Claus kept thinking of all the delicious food in the oven and couldn't swallow a spoonful.

At his feet under the table lay the sack with the horse hide in it. He stepped on the sack and the horse hide squeaked. 'Shhhhhhhh!' whispered Little Claus to the sack; but at the same time he pressed his foot down on it even harder and it squeaked even louder.

'What have you got in the bag?' asked the farmer.

'Oh, it's only a wizard,' Little Claus replied. 'He was telling me that there's no reason for us to eat porridge when he has just conjured both fish and meat for us, and even a cake. Look in the oven.'

'What!' exclaimed the farmer; and he ran to the oven and opened it. There he saw all the good food that his wife had made for the deacon; and she – not daring to tell him the truth – silently served the roast, the fish, and the cake.

After he had taken a few mouthfuls, Little Claus stepped on the sack again so that the hide squeaked.

'What is the wizard saying now?' asked the farmer eagerly.

'He says that he has conjured three bottles of wine for us and that you will find them in the corner next to the oven.'

The farmer's poor wife brought out the wine, which she had hidden, and poured it for Little Claus and her husband, who made so many toasts to each other's health that they were soon very merry. Then the farmer began to think about Little Claus's sack and what a wonderful thing it must be to have a wizard.

'Do you think he could conjure the Devil?' the farmer asked. 'For now that I have the courage I wouldn't mind seeing what he looks like.'

'Why not?' replied Little Claus. 'My wizard will do anything I tell him to . . . Won't you?' he added, stepping on the sack so that it squeaked. Turning to the farmer, Little Claus smiled. 'Can't you hear that he said yes? But the Devil has such an ugly face that he's not worth looking at.'

'I'm not afraid,' said the farmer, and hiccupped. 'How terrible can he look?'

'He looks just like a deacon!'

'Pooh!' returned the farmer. 'That's worse than I thought! I must confess that I cannot stand the sight of a deacon; but now that I know that it is only the Devil I will be looking at, maybe I can bear it. But don't let him come too near me and let's get it over with before I lose my courage.'

'I'll tell my wizard,' said Little Claus and stepped on the hide; then he cocked his head as if he were listening to someone.

'What is he saying?' asked the farmer, who could only hear the hide squeak.

'He says that if we go over to the chest in the corner and open it up we shall see the Devil sitting inside. But we must be careful when we lift the lid, not to lift it too high, so the Devil can escape.'

'Then you must hold on to the lid while I lift it,' whispered the farmer to Little Claus as he tiptoed to the chest in which the deacon was hiding. This poor fellow had heard every word that Little Claus and the farmer had said and was quaking with fear.

The farmer opened the chest no more than an inch or two and peeped inside. 'Ah!' he screamed and jumped up, letting the lid fall back into place. 'I saw him! He looked exactly like our deacon! It was a dreadful sight!'

After such an experience you need a drink; and Little Claus and the farmer had many, for they drank late into the night.

'You must sell me that wizard,' the farmer finally said. 'Ask whatever you want for it . . . I'll give you a bushel basket full of money, if that's what you'd like.'

'I wouldn't think of it,' replied Little Claus. 'You have seen for yourself all the marvellous things that wizard can do.'

'But I want it with all my heart,' begged the farmer; and he kept on pleading with Little Claus until at last he agreed.

'I cannot forget that you gave me a night's lodging,' Little Claus said. 'Take my wizard, but remember to fill the bushel basket to the very top.'

'I shall! I shall!' exclaimed the farmer. 'But you must take the chest along too. I won't have it in my house. Who knows but that the Devil isn't still inside it?'

And that's how it happened that Little Claus gave the

farmer a sack with a horse hide in it and in return was given not only a bushel full of money and a chest but a wheelbarrow to carry them away.

'Good-bye!' called Little Claus, and off he went.

On the other side of the forest there was a deep river with a current that flowed so swiftly that you could not swim against it. But the river had to be crossed and so a bridge had been built. When Little Claus reached the middle of that bridge, he said very loudly – so the deacon, who was still inside the chest, could hear him – 'What's the point of dragging this chest any farther? It's so heavy, you'd think it was filled with stones. I'm all worn out. I know what I'll do, I'll dump the chest into the stream and if the current carries it home to me, all well and good; and if not, it doesn't matter.' Then he took hold of the chest and pushed it, as if he were about to lift it out of the wheelbarrow and let it fall into the water.

'No, stop it!' cried the deacon from inside the chest. 'Let me out! Please, let me out!'

'Oh!' shouted Little Claus as if he were frightened. 'The Devil is still in there. I'd better throw the chest right into the river and drown him.'

'No! No!' screamed the deacon. 'I'll give you a bushel of money if you'll let me out!'

 'That's a different tune,' said Little Claus, and opened

the chest. The deacon climbed out and shoved the chest into the river. Together Little Claus and the deacon went to the deacon's home, where he gave Little Claus the bushel of coins that he had promised him. Now Little Claus had a whole wheelbarrow full of money.

'That wasn't bad payment for my old horse,' he said to himself as he dumped all the coins out on the floor of his own living room. 'What a big pile it is! It will annoy Big Claus to find out how rich I have become, all because of my horse. I won't tell him but let him find out for himself.'

A few minutes later a boy banged on Big Claus's door and asked him if he could borrow his grain measure for Little Claus.

'I wonder what he is going to use that for,' thought Big Claus; and in order to find out he dabbed a bit of tar in the bottom of the measuring pail, which was quite clever of him because when it was returned he found a silver coin stuck to the spot.

'Where did that come from?' shouted Big Claus, and ran as fast as he could to Little Claus's house. When he saw Little Claus in the midst of his riches, he shouted even louder, 'Where did you get all that money from?'

'Oh, that was for my horse hide, I sold it last night.'

'You were certainly well paid!' said Big Claus; and hurried home where he took an axe and killed all four of his horses; then he flayed them and set off for town with their hides.

'Hides for sale! Hides for sale! Who wants to buy hides?' Big Claus shouted from street to street.

All the shoemakers and tanners came out of their workshops to ask him the price of his wares.

'A bushel full of coins for each hide,' he replied.

'You must be mad!' they all shouted at once. 'Do you think we count money by the bushel?'

'Hides for sale! Hides for sale!' Big Claus repeated. And every time that someone asked him the price he said again, 'A bushel full of coins.'

'Are you trying to make fools of us?' the shoemakers and the tanners shouted. And while the crowd continued to gather around them, the tanners took their leather aprons and the shoemakers their straps and began to beat Big Claus.

'Hides . . .' screamed one of the tanners. 'We'll see to it that your hide spits red!'

'Out of town with him!' they shouted. And certainly Big Claus did his best to get out of town as fast as he could; never in his whole life had he had such a beating.

'Little Claus is going to pay for this!' he decided when he got home. 'He is going to pay with his life.'

But while Big Claus was in town, something unfortunate

had occurred: Little Claus's grandmother had died. And although she had been a very mean and scolding hag, who had never been kind to Little Claus, he felt very sad. Thinking that it might bring her back to life, he put his old grandmother in his own warm bed and decided to let her stay there all night, even though this meant that he would have to sleep in a chair.

It was not the first time that Little Claus had tried sleeping in a chair, but he could not sleep anyway; so he was wide awake when Big Claus came and tiptoed across the room to the bed in which he thought Little Claus was sleeping.

With an axe Big Claus hit the old grandmother on top of the head as hard as he could. 'That's what you get for making a fool of me,' he explained. 'And now you won't be able to do it again,' he, added and went home.

'What a wicked man!' thought Little Claus. 'If my grandmother hadn't already been dead, he would have killed her.'

Very early the next morning he dressed his grandmother in her Sunday best; then he borrowed a horse from his neighbour and harnessed it to his cart. On the small seat in the back of the cart, he put the old woman in a sitting position with bundles on either side of her, so she wouldn't fall out of the cart while he was driving. He went through the forest and just as the sun was rising he reached an inn. 'I'd better stop to get something to keep me alive,' he said.

It was a large inn, and the innkeeper was very rich. He was also very kind, but he had a ferocious temper, as if he had nothing inside him but pepper and tobacco.

'Good morning,' he said to Little Claus. 'You're dressed very finely for so early in the morning.'

'I'm driving to town with my grandmother,' he replied. 'She's sitting out in the cart because I couldn't persuade her to come in here with me. I wonder if you would be so kind as to take a glass of mead out to her; but speak a little loudly because she is a bit hard of hearing.'

'No sooner said than done,' answered the innkeeper; and he poured a large glass of mead which he carried out to the dead woman.

'Here is a glass of mead, which your son ordered for you,' said the innkeeper loudly but politely; but the dead woman sat perfectly still and said not a word.

'Can't you hear me?' he shouted. 'Here is mead from your son!'

He shouted the same words again as loud as he could, and still the old woman sat staring straight ahead. The more he shouted, the madder the innkeeper got, until finally he lost his temper and threw the mead, glass and all, right into the woman's face. With the mead dripping down her nose, she fell over backwards, for Little Claus had not tied her to the seat.

'What have you done?' shouted Little Claus as he flung open the door of the inn. 'Why, you have killed my grandmother!' he cried, grabbing the innkeeper by the shirt. 'Look at the wound she has on her head!'

'Oh, what a calamity!' the innkeeper exclaimed, and wrung his hands. 'It is all because of that temper of mine! Sweet, good Little Claus, I will give you a bushel full of money and bury your grandmother as if she were my own, as long as you'll keep quiet about what really happened, because if you don't they'll chop my head off; and that's so nasty.'

And that was how Little Claus got another bushel full of coins; and the innkeeper, true to his word, buried the old woman as well as he would have had she been his own grandmother.

As soon as he got home Little Claus sent his boy to borrow Big Claus's grain measure.

'What, haven't I killed him?' Big Claus exclaimed. 'I must find out what's happened. I'll take the measure over there myself.'

When he arrived at Little Claus's and saw all the money, his eyes grew wide with wonder and greed. 'Where did you get all that from?' he demanded.

'It was my grandmother and not me that you killed, and now I have sold her body for a bushel full of money.'

'You were certainly well paid,' said Big Claus, and hurried home. When he got there he took an axe and killed his old grandmother; then he dumped the poor old woman's body in his carriage and drove into town. He went at once to the apothecary and asked if he wanted to buy a corpse.

'Who is it and where did you get it from?' the apothecary inquired.

'Oh, it is my grandmother and I have killed her so I could sell her body for a bushel of money,' Big Claus said.

'God save us!' cried the apothecary. 'You don't know what you're saying . . . If you talk like that, you'll lose your head.' And the apothecary lectured him, telling him how wicked a crime murder was and that it was committed only by the most evil of men, who deserved the severest punishment. Big Claus was terrified and leaped into his carriage. He set off in the direction of his home, wildly whipping his horses. But no one tried to stop him, for everyone believed that he had gone mad.

'I'll make you pay for this!' Big Claus cried as soon as he was well out of town. 'Little Claus is going to pay for this,' he repeated when he got home. Then he took a large sack and went to see Little Claus.

 'So you fooled me again!' he shouted. 'First I killed my

horses and then my grandmother; and it's all your fault. But you have fooled me for the last time!' Grabbing Little Claus around the waist, he shoved him into the sack. As he flung the sack over his shoulder he said loudly, 'And now I am going to drown you!'

It was quite far to the river, and as he walked the sack with Little Claus in it seemed to grow heavier and heavier. The road went past the church, and Big Claus heard the organ being played and the congregation singing. 'It would be nice to hear a hymn or two before I go on,' he thought. 'Everybody's in church and Little Claus can't get out of the sack.' So Big Claus put down the sack near the entrance and went into the church.

'Poor me! Poor me!' sighed Little Claus. He twisted and turned but he could not loosen the cord that had been tied around the opening of the sack.

At that moment an old herdsman happened to pass. He had snow-white hair and walked with a long crook. In front of him he drove a large herd of cows and bulls. One of the bulls bumped into the sack and Little Claus was turned over.

'Poor me! Poor me!' cried Little Claus. 'I am so young and am already bound for Heaven.'

'Think of poor me; I am an old man,' said the herdsman, 'and am not allowed to enter it.'

'Open up the sack!' shouted Little Claus. 'You get

inside it, instead of me, and then you will get to Heaven right away!'

'Nothing could be better,' said the old man. He untied the sack and Little Claus crawled out at once.

'Take good care of my cattle,' the herdsman begged as he climbed into the sack. Little Claus promised that he would and tied the sack securely. Then he went on his way, driving the herd before him.

A little later Big Claus came out of the church and lifted the sack on to his back. He was surprised how much lighter it was now, for the old man weighed only half as much as Little Claus.

'How easy it is to carry now; it did do me good to hear a hymn!' he thought.

Big Claus went directly down to the river that was both deep and wide and dumped the sack into the water, shouting after it: 'You have made a fool of me for the last time!' For of course he believed that Little Claus was still inside the sack that was disappearing into the river.

On his way home he met Little Claus with all his cattle at the crossroads.

'What!' exclaimed Big Claus. 'Haven't I drowned you?'

'Oh yes,' answered Little Claus, 'You threw me in the river about half an hour ago.'

'But where did you get that huge herd of cattle?' Big Claus demanded.

'They are river cattle,' replied Little Claus. 'I'll tell you everything that happened to me. But, by the way, first I want to thank you for drowning me. For now I shall never have anything to worry about again, I am really rich . . . Believe me, I was frightened when you threw me over the bridge. The wind whistled in my ears as I fell into the cold water. I sank straight to the bottom; but I didn't hurt myself because I landed on the softest, most beautiful green grass you can imagine. Then the sack was opened by the loveliest maiden. She was all dressed in white except for the green wreath in her wet hair. Taking my hand, she asked, "Aren't you Little Claus?" When I nodded she said, "Here are some cattle for you and six miles up the road there is an even bigger herd waiting for you." Then I realized that to the water people the streams and rivers were as roads are to us. They use them to travel on. Far from their homes under the oceans, they follow the streams and the rivers until they finally become too shallow and come to an end. There are the most beautiful flowers growing down there and the finest freshest grass; the fish swimming around above your head remind you of the birds flying in the air. The people are as nice as they can be; and the cattle fat and friendly.'

'Then tell me why you came up here on land again,' said Big Claus. 'I never would have left a place as wonderful as that.'

'Well,' said Little Claus, 'that is just because I am smart. I told you that the water maiden said that another herd of cattle would be waiting for me six miles up the road. By "road" she meant the river; and I am eager to see my cattle. You know how the river twists and turns while the road up here on land is straight; so I thought that if I used the road instead of the river I would get there much faster and save myself at least two miles of walking.'

'Oh, you are a lucky man!' exclaimed Big Claus. 'Do you think that if I were thrown into the river, I would be given cattle too?'

'I don't know why not,' replied Little Claus. 'But I cannot carry you, as you did me, you're too heavy. But if you'll find a sack and climb into it yourself I'll be glad to go to the bridge with you and push you into the water.'

'Thank you very much,' said Big Claus. 'But if I don't get a herd of cattle when I get down there I'll beat you as you have never been beaten before.'

'Oh no! How can you think of being so mean!' whimpered Little Claus as they made their way to the river.

It was a hot day and when the cattle spied the water they started running towards it, for they were very thirsty. 'See how eager they are to get to the river,' remarked Little Claus. 'They are longing for their home under the water.'

'Never mind them!' shouted Big Claus. 'Or I'll give you a beating right here and now.' He grabbed a sack that was lying on one of the bulls' backs and climbed up on the bridge. 'Get a rock and put it in with me, I'm afraid that I might float.'

'Don't worry about that,' said Little Claus. But he found a big stone anyway and rolled it into the sack next to Big Claus before he tied the opening as tightly as he could. Then he pushed the sack off the bridge.

Splash! Plop! Down went Big Claus into the river and straight to the bottom he went.

'I am afraid that he will have trouble finding his cattle,' said Little Claus, and drove his own herd home.

The Flying Trunk

Once there was a merchant who was so rich that he could easily have paved a whole street with silver coins and still have had enough left over to pave a little alley as well. But he didn't do anything so foolish, he made better use of his money than that. He didn't give out a copper coin without getting a silver one in return; that's how good a merchant he was, but he couldn't live forever.

His son inherited all his money, and he was better at spending than at saving it. Every night he attended a party or a masquerade. He made kites out of bank notes; and when he went to the beach, he didn't skim stones; no, he skimmed gold coins. In that way, the money was soon gone, and finally he had nothing but four pennies, a pair of worn-out slippers, and an old dressing gown. He lost all his friends; they didn't like to be seen with a person so curiously dressed. But one of them was kind enough to give him an old trunk and say to him, 'Pack and get out.' That was all very well, but he had nothing to pack, so he sat down inside the trunk himself.

It was a strange trunk; if you pressed on the lock, then it could fly. That is what the merchant's son did, and away it carried him. Up through the chimney, up above the clouds and far, far away. The trunk creaked and groaned; its passenger was afraid that the bottom would fall out, for then he would have a nasty fall. But it didn't, the trunk flew him directly to the land of the Turks and landed.

The merchant's son hid the trunk beneath some leaves in a forest and started to walk into town. No one took any notice of him, for in Turkey everyone wears a dressing gown and slippers.

He met a nurse carrying a babe in her arms. 'Hey, you Turkish nurse,' he said, 'what kind of a castle is that one, right outside the city, with windows placed so high up the walls that no one but a giant could look through them?'

'That is where the princess lives,' replied the nurse. 'It has been prophesied that a lover will cause her great suffering and sorrow, that is why no one can visit her unless the king and the queen are present.'

'Thank you,' said the merchant's son. He ran back into the forest where he had hidden the trunk, climbed into it, and flew up to the roof of the palace; then he climbed through a window to the princess.

She was sleeping on a sofa and looked so beautiful that the merchant's son had to kiss her. She woke up and was terrified at the sight of the strange man, but he told her that he was the God of the Turks and that he had come flying through the air to visit her. That story didn't displease her.

They sat next to each other on the settee and he told her stories. He made up one about her eyes being the loveliest dark forest pools in which thoughts swam like mermaids. He told her that her forehead was a snow mountain filled with grand halls, whose walls were covered with beautiful paintings. And he told her about the storks that bring such sweet little children. Oh, they were delightful stories; then he proposed and she said yes.

'Come back on Saturday,' she said, 'then the king and queen come for afternoon tea. They will be proud that I am going to marry the God of the Turks. But make sure, sir, that you have some good fairy tales to tell them. My mother likes noble and moral stories, and my father lively ones that can make him laugh.'

'Stories are the only wedding gift I shall bring,' said the merchant's son, and smiled most pleasingly. Before they parted the princess gave him a sword with a whole lot of gold coins attached to the hilt; and these he was in need of.

The merchant's son flew away and bought himself a new dressing gown. When he returned to the forest he started to compose the fairy tale that he would tell on

Saturday. And that wasn't so easy. But finally he was finished and Saturday came.

The king, the queen, and the whole court were having tea with the princess. They greeted him most kindly.

'Now you must tell us a fairy tale,' said the queen, 'and I want it to be both profound and instructive.'

'But at the same time funny,' added the king.

'I will try,' said the merchant's son.

Here is his story; if you listen carefully, you will understand it.

Once upon a time there were some sulphur matches who were extremely proud because they came of such good family. Their family tree, of which each of them was a tiny splinter, had been the largest pine tree in the forest. The matches lay on a shelf between a tinderbox and an old iron pot; and to them they told the story of their childhood and youth.

Then we lived high, so to speak. We were served diamond tea every morning and evening; it is called dew. Whenever the sun was out it shone upon us, and all the little birds had to tell us stories. We knew that we were rich, for we could afford to wear our green clothes all year round, whereas the poor beeches and oaks had to stand quite naked in the winter and freeze. Then the woodcutter came, it was a revolution! The whole family was split. The trunk of our family tree got a job as the mainmast on a full-rigged ship; he can sail around the whole world if he feels like it. We are not sure what happened to the branches, but we got the job of lighting fires for the mean and base multitudes; that is how such noble and aristocratic things as we are ended up in the kitchen.'

'My life has been quite different,' said the iron pot that stood on the shelf beside the matches. 'From my very birth, I have been scrubbed and set over the fire to boil. I have lost count of how many times that has happened. I do the solid, the most important work here, and should be counted first among you all. My only diversion is to stand properly cleaned on the shelf and engage in a dignified conversation with my friends. We are all proper stay-at-homes here, except for the water bucket, which does run down to the well every so often, and the market basket. She brings us news from the town, but as far as I am concerned it is all disagreeable. All she can talk about are the people and the government. Why, the other day an old earthen pot got so frightened that it fell down and broke in pieces. The market basket is a liberal!'

'You talk too much!' grumbled the tinderbox. 'Let us have a pleasant evening.' And the steel struck the flint so that sparks flew.

'Yes, let us discuss who is the most important person here,' suggested the matches.

'I don't like to talk about myself,' said an earthenware pot. 'Let's tell stories instead. I will begin with an everyday story, the kind that could have happened to any of us. I think that kind of story is the most amusing: *By the Baltic Sea where the Danish beeches mirror their* –'

'That is a beautiful beginning,' exclaimed the plates. 'We are sure we will love that story.'

'*There I spent my youth in a quiet home,*' continued the earthenware pot. '*The furniture was polished each week, the floors washed every second day, and the curtains were washed and ironed every fortnight.*'

'How interestingly you describe it,' interrupted the feather duster. 'One can hear that a woman is talking, there is an air of cleanliness about it all.'

'How true, how true!' said the water bucket, and jumped, out of pure joy, several inches into the air.

The earthenware pot told its story; and both the middle and the end were just as interesting as the beginning had been.

All the plates clattered in unison as applause, and the feather duster took some parsley and made it into a garland with which to crown the pot. She knew it would irritate the others; besides, she thought, 'If I honour her today, she will honour me tomorrow.'

'We will dance,' said the big black pair of tongs; and so they did! Goodness, how they could stretch their legs.

The cover on the old chair, over in the corner, split right down the middle just trying to follow them with his eyes. 'Where are our laurel leaves?' demanded the tongs when they had finished; and they were crowned with a garland too.

'Vulgar rabble,' thought the matches; but they didn't say it out loud.

The samovar was going to sing; but she had caught cold – at least so she claimed, but it wasn't true. She was too proud; she would only sing in the dining room, when the master and mistress were present.

Over on the window sill was an old pen that the maid used to write with. There was nothing special about it except that it had been dipped a little too deeply in the inkwell. The pen thought that this was a distinction and was proud of it. 'If the sanovar won't sing,' remarked the pen, 'we shouldn't beg it to. Outside the window hangs a bird cage with a nightingale in it; why not let him sing? True, his voice is untrained and he is quite uneducated; but his song has a pleasing naïve simplicity about it.'

'I object. I think it is most improper,' complained the teakettle, who was a half sister of the samovar. 'Why should we listen to a foreign bird? Is that patriotic? Let the market basket judge between us.'

 'I am annoyed and irritated,' shouted the market basket.

'It is most aggravating; what a way to spend an evening! Let's put everything back in its right place, then I'll rule the roost, as I ought to. And you'll see what a difference that will make.'

'Let's make noise! Let's make noise!' screamed all the others.

At that moment the door opened and the maid entered. Instantly, they stood still and kept quiet, every one of them. But even the smallest earthenware pot thought to herself, 'I am really the most important person here in the kitchen and, if I had wanted to, I could have made it into a most amusing evening.'

The maid took a match, struck it, and, lighted the fire. 'Now everyone can see,' thought the match, 'that we are the true aristocrats here. What a flame we make. What glorious light!' And that was the end of the match, it burned out.

'That was a lovely fairy tale,' said the queen. 'I feel just as if I had been in the kitchen with the matches. You shall have our daughter.'

'Certainly,' said the king. 'We will hold the wedding on Monday,' and he patted the merchant's son on the back, for now he was part of the family.

On Sunday evening the whole town was illuminated in honour of the impending marriage. Buns and pretzels were given away to everyone; and the street urchins whistled through their fingers. It was a moving sight.

'I'd better add to the festivities,' thought the merchant's son. He went out and bought all the fireworks he could, put them in the trunk, and flew up in the air.

Ah! How high he flew and the fireworks sputtered, glittered, and banged. Such a spectacle no one had seen before. All the Turks jumped a foot up into the air and lost their slippers. Now they knew it was the God of the Turks who would be marrying their princess.

When the merchant's son had returned in his trunk to the forest, he decided to go back into town in order to hear what everyone was saying about his performance – and it's quite understandable that he should want to.

And the things that people said! Everyone had seen something different, but they all agreed that it was marvellous.

'I saw the God himself,' said one man. 'He had eyes like stars and a beard like the foaming ocean.'

'He flew wearing a cloak of fire,' said another, 'and the prettiest cherubs were peeping out from under its folds.'

It was all very pleasing to hear; and tomorrow was his wedding day!

He hurried back to the forest to sleep the night away in his trunk. But where was it?

It had burned to ashes. A little spark from one of the

fireworks had ignited it; and that was the end of the trunk, and the merchant's son too! Now he could not fly to his bride.

She waited for him on the roof all day. She is still waiting for him, while he is wandering around the world, telling fairy tales; but they are not so lighthearted as the one he told about the sulphur matches.

The Bottle

In a crooked alley, among other ill-repaired houses, stood one that was particularly narrow and tall. It was a half-timbered house, and many of the beams were rotten. Only very poor people lived there. Outside the garret window hung a bird cage; it was as decrepit as the house, and its inhabitant did not even have a proper bath: the neck of a broken bottle, corked and hung upside down, had to suffice. The old maid who lived in the garret was standing by the open window, enjoying the warm sunshine. She had just fed the little linnet, and the songbird was hopping back and forth in the cage, singing merrily.

'Yes, you may sing,' said the bottleneck. It didn't really speak, for bottlenecks can't talk, but it thought all this inside itself, as we all do sometimes. 'Yes, you can sing. You are healthy and well, not an invalid like me. You don't know what it's like to lose your whole lower parts and be left with only a neck and mouth and then, on top of it, to have a cork stuffed into you. Then you wouldn't sing so loud! But it is good that someone is happy. I have nothing to sing about, and I can't sing. But I have lived an exciting life! I remember when the tanner took me along on a picnic and his daughter got engaged. I was a whole and proper bottle then. Goodness me, it seems just like yesterday . . . Oh yes, I have experienced a lot. I was created in fire and heat, have sailed across the ocean, lain in the dark earth, and been higher up in the sky than most people. Now I am perched above the street in the sunshine; yes, my story bears repeating. But I am not going to tell it out loud, because I can't.'

But the bottleneck could reminisce and it did. The bird sang, and the passers-by down in the alley thought about their own problems or didn't think at all, while the bottleneck reflected upon its life.

It remembered the great oven in the factory, where it had been blown into life. As soon as it had been formed, while it was still burning hot, it had been able to look into the burning red oven. It had felt a desire to jump back into it and be melted down again, but as it cooled that fancy had disappeared. The bottle had stood in a row together with all his sisters and brothers; there had been a whole regiment of them. They had all come from the same oven, but some had been blown into champagne bottles and others into beer bottles, and that makes a difference. Although later on, after they have come out into the world and the beer or the champagne has been drunk, then a beer bottle can be refilled with the costly wine from Vesuvius, Lachryma Christi, and the champagne bottle with boot blacking. But birth still counts and that you can tell from the shape. Nobility remains nobility, even when it contains only boot blacking.

All the bottles were put into cases, and so was the bottle that this story is about. It never occurred to him then that he would end as a useless bottleneck, and then have to work his way up to becoming a bird bath – for that is better than being nothing at all.

He saw daylight again when the cases of bottles were unpacked in the wine merchant's cellar. Now he was rinsed for the first time, that was a strange experience; then he was put on a shelf. There he lay empty and without a cork; he felt awkward; something was missing but he did not know quite what it was. Then the bottle was filled with wine, corked, and sealed. A label was pasted on it which said 'very fine quality'. The bottle felt as though he had passed an examination and received the highest grade. The wine was young and the bottle was young and the young tend to be lyrical. All sorts of songs about things, that the bottle couldn't possibly know a thing about, seemed to be humming inside him. He saw clearly the green sunlit mountains, where the grapes had grown, as well as the maidens and young men who had kissed each other while they picked the fruit. Oh yes, it is lovely to live! The bottle was filled with passion and love, just as young poets are before they know much about either.

One morning the bottle was sold. The tanner's apprentice had been sent down to buy a flask of the 'very best wine'. It was put into the picnic basket together with ham, cheese, sausage, the best-quality butter, and the finest bread. It was the tanner's daughter who packed the basket. She was young and lovely, with a smile in her brown eyes and laughter on her lips. Her hands were soft and white, but the skin on her neck was even whiter. She was one of the most beautiful girls in the town and not yet engaged.

She had the picnic basket basket on her lap, while they drove out into the forest. The bottle peeped out through the snowy white tablecloth that covered the basket; his cork was covered by red sealing wax. He could look right into the face of the young girl and he saw, too, the young seaman who was sitting beside her. They had been friends since childhood. He was the son of a portrait painter. He had just received his mate's licence and was to sail the following day on a long voyage to foreign lands. While preparing the basket for the picnic they had talked about the voyage, and there had been no joy or laughter to be seen in the young girl's face.

When they arrived in the forest the young couple went for a walk alone, and what did they talk about? Well, the bottle never knew, for he had stayed in the picnic basket. A very long time seemed to pass before he was taken out. But when it finally happened, something very pleasant seemed to have taken place. Everyone was smiling and laughing, the tanner's daughter too. She didn't say much, but two red roses were blooming on her cheeks.

The tanner took out his corkscrew and grabbed the bottle! It was a strange experience to be opened for the first time. The bottleneck had never forgotten that solemn moment when the cork was drawn and the wine streamed into the glasses.

'To the engaged couple!' toasted the tanner. They all emptied their glasses, and the young mate kissed his bride-to-be.

'Happiness and contentment!' exclaimed the old couple to the young.

The glasses were filled once more. 'A happy homecoming and a wedding, a year from now!' shouted the young man. When they had drunk this toast, he grasped the now empty bottle. 'You have been part of the happiest day of my life, you shall serve no one after that!'

The young mate threw the bottle high into the air. The tanner's daughter followed it with her eyes; she could not know then that she would see the very same bottle fly through the air once more during her life. The bottle landed in a little pond in the woods. The bottleneck remembered it all very clearly; he could even recall what he had thought when he lay in the water! 'I gave them wine, and they gave me swamp water in return, but they meant well.' The poor bottle could no longer see the picnic party, but heard them laughing and singing. Finally two little peasant boys came by, looked in among the reeds, noticed the bottle, picked it up; and now he had an owner again.

In the house in the woods, the eldest son had been home the day before; he was a seaman and was about to set out on a long voyage. His mother was making a package of one thing and another that she thought might be useful on so long a journey. His father would take it to the ship and give it to the lad together with his parents' blessings. A little bottle of homemade liquor had already been filled; but when the boys entered with the larger and stronger bottle, the woman decided to put the liquor in that one instead. It was brewed from herbs and was especially good for the stomach. So the bottle was filled once more, this time not with red wine but with bitter medicine, and that was of the 'very best' quality too.

Lying between a sausage and a cheese, it was delivered to Peter Jensen, who was the elder brother of the two boys who had found the bottle. Now the ship's mate was the very young man who had just become engaged to the tanner's daughter. He did not see the bottle; and if he had, he would not have recognized it, or imagined that the very bottle that had contained the wine with which he had toasted to a happy homecoming could be on board his ship.

True, the bottle was no longer filled with wine, but what it contained was just as desirable to Peter Jensen and his friends. They called Peter the 'apothecary', for it was he who doled out the medicine that cured stomach-aches so pleasantly. Yes, that was a good period in the bottle's life but at last it was empty.

It had stood forgotten in a corner a long time; then the terrible tragedy occurred. Whether it happened on the journey out or on the return voyage was never clear to the bottle, since he had not gone ashore. The ship was caught in the midst of a storm; great heavy black waves broke over the railing and lifted and tossed the vessel; the mast broke; and a plank in the hull was pressed loose. The water poured in so fast that it was useless to try to pump it out. It was a dark night. In the last few minutes before the ship sank, the young mate wrote on a piece of paper, 'In Jesus' name, we are lost.' Then he added the name of the ship, his own name, and that of his sweetheart. He put the sheet of paper into an empty bottle he had found, corked it, and threw it into the raging sea. He did not know that he had once before held that bottle in his hands, on the day of his engagement.

The ship sank, the crew was lost, but the bottle floated like a gull on the waves. Now that he had a sad love letter inside him, he had a heart. The bottle watched the sun rise and set, thought that the red disc was like the opening of the oven in which he had been born; he longed to float right into it. Days of calm were followed by a storm. The bottle was not broken against a cliff-bound shore, nor was it swallowed by a shark.

For years it drifted, following the currents of the ocean towards the north and then towards the south. He was his own master, but that, too, can become tiresome in the long run.

The note, the last farewell from a bridegroom to his bride, would only bring pain if ever it were held by the hand it had been meant for. Where were they now, those little white hands that had spread the tablecloth on the green moss the day of the picnic? Where was the tanner's daughter? Where was the country where it had happened? The bottle didn't know, he just drifted with the waves and the wind. Although he was thoroughly tired of it; after all, that wasn't what he was meant for. He had no choice in the matter, but finally he floated to shore. It was a foreign country, the bottle didn't understand a word of what was said; and that was most irritating. You miss so much when you don't understand the language.

The bottle was picked up, opened, and the note was taken out to be read. But the finder did not understand what was written on it; he turned the note both upside down and right side up, but he could not read it. He realized that the bottle had been thrown overboard and that the note was a message from a ship, but what it said remained a mystery to him. The note was put back in the bottle and the bottle put away in a closet.

Every time there were visitors the note was shown in the hope that someone could read it, but no one who came ever could. The note that had been written with pencil was made less and less legible by the many hands that held it. Finally the letters could no longer be seen and the bottle was put up in the attic. Spider webs and dust covered him, while he dreamed about the past: the good old days when he had been filled with wine and had been taken on a picnic. Even the days on the ocean seemed pleasant now; the years when he had floated on the sea and had had a secret inside him: a letter, a sigh of farewell.

It remained in the attic twenty years and would have stayed there even longer had not the owner decided to enlarge his house. The whole roof was torn down. The bottle was brought out and the story of how it was found told once more. The bottle did not understand what was being said, for you don't learn a language by standing twenty years in an attic. 'If only they had allowed me to stay in the closet downstairs, then I would probably have learned it,' thought the bottle.

Once more he was washed and rinsed – and he certainly needed it. The bottle was so clean and transparent that he felt young in his old age; but the note had been lost in the process.

Now the bottle was filled up with seeds: what kind they were the bottle didn't know. Again he was corked, and then wrapped in paper so tightly that not a bit of light came through. He could see neither the sun nor the moon; and the bottle felt that this was a great shame, for what is the point of travelling if you don't see anything? But travel it did and it arrived safely at its destination and was unpacked.

'They certainly have been careful' – the bottle heard someone say – 'but I suppose it has broken anyway.' But the bottle was whole, and he understood every word that was said. They spoke his own language, the first one he had heard when he came red-hot out of the melting pot: the language that had been spoken at the wine merchant's, at the picnic, and on the ship – his native tongue, the one he understood! The bottle had come home!. Oh, what a lovely welcome sound! The bottle nearly jumped for pure joy out of the hands that had picked him up. He hardly felt the cork being drawn and the seeds being shaken out, so happy was he!

He was put down in a cellar, again to be hidden and forgotten by the world. But it's good to be home even when one has to stay in the cellar. The bottle did not even count the years and days he stayed there. Finally somebody came and removed all the bottles, himself included.

The garden outside the house had been decorated. Coloured lamps hung from all the trees and bushes; they looked like shining tulips. It was a lovely evening, perfectly still, and the sky was filled with stars. There was a new moon, a tiny sliver of silver surrounding a pale disc; it was a beautiful sight for those who look at beauty.

The paths at the edges of the garden were illuminated too – at least, enough for you to find your way. In the spaces between the bushes of the hedge, bottles with candles in them had been placed. Here, too, stood the bottle that was fated to end as a birdbath. He found the whole affair marvellously to his taste; here he stood, among the greenery, attending a party; he could hear laughter and music and all the sounds of gaiety. True, it came mostly from another part of the garden, where the coloured lamps were hung. He had been placed in the more lonesome area; but that gave the bottle more time for reflection. He felt that he stood there not only for amusement and beauty but also because he was useful. Such a combination is superior and can make one forget the twenty years one has spent in the attic – that sort of thing it is best to forget.

A young couple came walking by, arm in arm, just as

the other young couple, on the day of the picnic, had: the tanner's daughter and the mate from the ship. The bottle felt that he was reliving something that had happened once before. Among the guests were some who had not really been invited but were allowed to come and look at the festivities. One of these was an old maid; she had no kin but she had friends. She was having exactly the same thoughts as the bottle; she was also recalling an afternoon spent in the woods, and a young couple walking arm in arm. She had been half of that sight and those had been the happiest moments of her life, and they are not forgotten, regardless of how old one becomes. She did not recognize the bottle nor he her.

That is the way of the world, we can pass each other unnoticed until we are introduced to each other again. And those two were to meet once more, now that they lived in the same town.

From the garden, the bottle was taken to the wine merchant, rinsed, and then once more filled with wine. It was sold to a balloonist, who, on the following Sunday, was to ascend into the sky in a balloon. A great crowd of people gathered to see the event and the regimental band played. The battle saw all the preparations for the air voyage from a basket, where he lay together with a rabbit who was to be dropped down with a parachute on. The poor bunny, who knew its fate, looked anything but happy. The balloon grew and grew and finally rose from the ground when it couldn't grow any fatter; then the ropes that held it down were cut and it slowly ascended into the sky, carrying the basket with the balloonist, the bottle, and the frightened rabbit up into the air. The crowd below cheered and screamed: 'Hurrah!'

'It is a strange feeling,' thought the bottle. 'It is another way of sailing but, at least, up here you can't run aground.'

Many thousands of people were watching the balloon and the old maid in the garret was looking at it too. She was standing at her window, where the bird cage with the little songbird hung; at that time it did not have a glass birdbath but only a cracked cup that had lost its handle. On the window sill was a myrtle bush; the flowerpot had been moved a little out of the way so that the woman could lean out of the window and get a better view of the balloon.

She could see everything clearly: how the balloonist threw the rabbit out and its tiny parachute unfolded.

Now he was taking the bottle and uncorking it. He drank a toast to all the spectators. But he did not put the bottle back; instead he cast it high into the air. The old maid saw that too, but she did not know that this was the very bottle she had seen fly once before: in the spring-time of her life, on that happy day in the green forest.

The bottle had hardly the time to think half a thought, not to speak of a whole one. The high point of his life had come and so unexpectedly! Far below him were the towers and roofs of the city; the people looked so tiny.

The bottle descended at quite a different speed than the rabbit had. The bottle performed somersaults as he fell; he had been half filled with wine, but soon that was gone. He felt so young, so joyful and gay. What a journey! The sun reflected in him and every person below was following him with their eyes.

The balloon was soon out of sight and so was the bottle; it fell on a roof and splintered. It hit with such force that all the little pieces danced and jumped, and did not rest before they had fallen all the way down into a yard. The neck of the bottle was whole; it looked as if it had been cut from the rest of the bottle with a diamond.

'It would do as a birdbath,' said the man who found it. He lived in a cellar. But since he had neither cage nor bird, he thought it a little expensive to buy them just because he had an old bottleneck that could be used as a birdbath. He remembered the old maid who lived up under the roof, she might find it useful.

A cork was put in the bottleneck and it was hung upside down in the cage of the little bird that sang so beautifully. Now it was filled with fresh water instead of wine; and what used to be 'up' was 'down', but that is the sort of change that sometimes does happen in this world.

'Yes, you can sing,' sighed the bottleneck, who had had so many adventures. The bird and the old maid knew only of the most recent one when he had been up in a balloon.

Now the bottle had become a birdbath; he could hear the rumble of the traffic down in the street and the voice of the mistress talking to an old friend. They were not talking about the bottleneck but about the myrtle bush in the window.

'There is no reason for you to spend two crowns on a bridal bouquet for your daughter,' the old maid was saying. 'I will cut you a beautiful one from my bush. You remember the myrtle bush you gave me the day after I had become engaged? Well, the little bush over in the window is a cutting from that one. You hoped that I would cut my bridal bouquet from it, but that day never came. Those eyes are closed that should have shone for me and been the happiness of my life. On the bottom of the sea he sleeps now, my beloved. The bush you gave me became old, but I became even older. When it was just about to die, I cut a branch from it and planted it. Look how it has thrived finally, it will attend a wedding: your daughter's.'

There were tears in the old woman's eyes as she talked about the young man who had loved her when she was young. She recalled his toast and the first kiss he had given her; but that she did not tell about, for she was truly an old maid. No matter how much she thought about the past, it never occurred to her that just outside the window, in the bird cage, hung a witness to those times: the neck of the very bottle that had contained the wine with which her engagement had been celebrated. The bottleneck did not recognize her either, nor did he listen to what she was saying, but that was mostly because the bottleneck never thought about anyone but himself.

The Girl Who Stepped on Bread

I suppose you have heard about the girl who stepped on the bread in order not to get her shoes dirty, and how badly she fared. The story has been both written down and printed.

She was a poor child, but proud and arrogant; she had what is commonly called a bad character. When she was very little it had given her pleasure to tear the wings off flies, so they forever after would have to crawl. If she caught a dung beetle, she would stick a pin through its body then place a tiny piece of paper where the poor creature's legs could grab hold of it; and watch the insect twist and turn the paper, round and round, in the vain hope that, with its help, it could pull itself free of the pin.

'Look, the dung beetle is reading,' little Inger – that was her name – would scream and laugh. 'Look, it is turning over the page.'

She did not improve as she grew up; in fact, she became worse. She was pretty, and that was probably her misfortune; otherwise, the world would have treated her rougher.

 'A strong brine is needed to scrub that head,' her own

mother said about her. 'You stepped on my apron when you were small, I am afraid you will step on my heart when you grow older.'

And she did!

A job was found for her as a maid in a house out in the country. The family she worked for was very distinguished and wealthy. Both her master and mistress treated her kindly, more as if she were their daughter than their servant. Pretty she was and prettily was she dressed, and prouder and prouder she became.

After she had been in service for a year her mistress said to her, 'You should go and visit your parents, little Inger.'

She went, but it was because she wanted to show off her fine dresses. When she came to the entrance of her village, near the little pond where the young men and girls were gossiping, she saw her mother sitting on a stone. The woman was resting, for she had been in the forest gathering wood, and a whole bundle of faggots lay beside her.

Inger was ashamed that she – who was so finely dressed – should have a mother who wore rags and had to collect sticks for her fire. The girl turned around and walked away, with irritation but no regret.

Half a year passed and her mistress said again, 'You should go home for the day and visit your old parents.

Here is a big loaf of white bread you can take along. I am sure they will be very happy to see you.'

Inger dressed in her very best clothes and put on her new shoes. She lifted her skirt a little as she walked and was very careful where she trod, so that she would not dirty or spoil her finery. That one must not hold against her; but when the path became muddy, and finally a big puddle blocked her way, she threw the bread into it rather than get her shoes wet. As she stepped on the bread, it sank deeper and deeper into the mud, carrying her with it, until she disappeared. At last, all that could be seen were a few dark bubbles on the surface of the puddle.

This is the manner in which the story is most often told. But what happened to the girl? Where did she disappear to? She came down to the bog witch! The bog witch is an aunt of the elves, on their father's side. The elves everyone knows. Poems have been written about them and they have been painted, too. But about the bog witch most people don't know very much.

When the mist lies over the swamps and bogs, one says, 'Look, the bog witch is brewing!' It was into this very brewery that Inger sank, and that is not a place where it is pleasant to stay. A cesspool is a splendidly light and airy room in comparison to the bog witch's brewery. The smell that comes from every one of the vats is so horrible that a human being would faint if he got even a whiff of it. The vats stand so close together that there is hardly room to walk between them, and if you do find a little space to squeeze through, then it is all filled with toads and slimy snakes. This is the place that Inger came to. The snakes and toads felt so cold against her body that she shivered and shook. But not for long. Inger felt her body grow stiffer and stiffer, until at last she was as rigid as a statue. The bread still stuck to her foot, there was no getting rid of it.

The bog witch was at home that day; the brewery was being inspected by the Devil's great-grandmother. She is an ancient and very venomous old lady who never wastes her time. When she leaves home, she always takes some needlework with her. That day she was embroidering lies and crocheting thoughtless words that she had picked up as they fell. Everything she does is harmful and destructive. She knows how to sew, embroider, and crochet well, that old great-grandmother!

She looked at Inger, and then took out her glasses and looked at her a second time. 'That girl has talent!' she declared. 'I would like to have her as a souvenir of my visit. She is worthy of a pedestal in the entrance hall of my great-grandson's palace.'

The bog witch gave Inger to the Devil's great-grandmother. And that is the way she went to hell. Most people go straight down there, but if you are as talented as Inger, then you can get there via a detour.

The Devil's entrance hall was an endless corridor that made you dizzy if you looked down it. Inger was not the only one to decorate this grand hall; the place was crowded with figures all waiting for the door of mercy to open for them, and they had long to wait. Around their feet, big fat spiders spun webs that felt like fetters and were as strong as copper chains, and they would last at least a thousand years. Every one of these immovable statues had a soul within it that was as restless as its body was rigid and stiff. The miser knew that he had forgotten the key to his money box in its lock, and he could do nothing about it. Oh, it would take me much too long to explain and describe all the torments and tortures that they went through. Inger felt how horrible it was to stand there as a statue, her foot locked to the bread.

'That is what one gets for trying to keep one's feet clean,' she said to herself. 'Look how they are all staring at me!' That was true, they were all looking at the latest arrival, and their evil desires were mirrored in their eyes and spoken without sound by their horrible lips. It was a monstrous sight!

'I, at least, am a pleasure to look at,' thought little Inger. 'I have a pretty face and pretty clothes on.' She moved her eyes; her neck was too stiff to turn. Goodness me, how dirty she was! She had forgotten all the filth and slime she had been through in the bog witch's brewery. All her clothes were so covered with mire that she looked as if she were dressed in mud. A snake had got into her hair and hung down her neck. And from the folds of her dress big toads looked up at her and barked like Pekinese dogs. It was all very unpleasant. But she comforted herself with the thought that the others didn't look any better than she did.

But far worse than all this was the terrible hunger she felt. She couldn't bend down and break off a piece of the bread she was stepping on. Her back was stiff and her arms and legs were stiff, her whole body was like a stone statue; only her eyes could move. They could turn all the way around, so that she looked inside herself and that, too, was an unpleasant sight. Then the flies came; they climbed all over her face, stepped back and forth across her eyes. She blinked to scare them away, but they couldn't fly; their wings had been torn off. That was painful too, but the hunger was worse. Inger felt as if her stomach had eaten itself. She became more and more empty inside, horribly empty.

'If this is going to last long, then I won't endure it!' she said to herself. But it didn't stop, it kept on; and she had to endure it.

A tear fell on her head, rolled down her face and chest,

and landed on the bread; and many more tears followed. Who was weeping because of little Inger? She had a mother up on earth, it was she who was weeping. Those tears that mothers shed in sorrow over their bad children always reach the children, but they do not help them, they only make their pain and misery greater. Oh, that terrible hunger did not cease. If only she could reach the bread she was stepping on. She felt as if everything inside her had eaten itself up, and she was a hollow shell in which echoed everything that was said about her up on earth. She could hear it all, and none of it was pleasant, every word was hard and condemning. Her mother wept over her, but she also said: 'Pride goes before a fall! That was your misfortune, Inger! How you have grieved your poor mother!'

Everyone up on earth – her mother, too – knew about the sin she had committed, how she had stepped on the bread and disappeared into the mire. A shepherd had seen it happen, and he had told everyone about it.

'You have made me so miserable, Inger!' sighed her mother. 'But that is what I expected would happen.'

'I wish I had never been born,' thought Inger. 'That would have been much better. But it doesn't help now that my mother cries.'

She heard her master and mistress, who had been like
 parents to her, talking. 'She was a sinful child,' they said.

'She did not appreciate God's gifts but stepped on them; it will not be easy for her to find grace.'

'They should have been stricter,' thought Inger, 'and shaken the nonsense out of me.'

She heard that a song had been made up about her, 'The haughty girl who stepped on the bread to keep her pretty shoes dry'. It was very popular, everyone in the country sang it.

'Imagine that, one has to have it thrown in one's face so often, and suffer so much for such a little sin,' thought Inger. 'The others should also be punished for their sins. Then there would be a lot to punish! Uh! How I suffer!'

And her soul became as hard as or even harder than her shell. 'How can one improve in such company as there is down here?' she thought. 'But I don't want to be good! Look how they stare!' And her soul was filled with hatred against all other human beings. 'Now they have something to talk about up there. Oh, how I suffer!'

Every time that her story was told to some little child, Inger could hear it and she never heard a kind word about herself, for children judge harshly. They would call her the 'ungodly Inger' and say that she was disgusting, and even declare that they were glad that she was punished.

But one day, as hunger and anger were tearing at her insides, she heard her story being told to a sweet, innocent little girl, and the child burst out crying. She wept for the haughty, finery-loving Inger. 'But won't she ever come up to earth again?' she asked.

And the grown-up who had told her the story said, 'No, she will never come up on earth again.'

'But if she said she was sorry and she would never do it again?'

'But she won't say she is sorry,' answered the grown-up.

'I wish she would,' cried the little girl. 'I would give my doll's house if she only could come back up on earth again. I think it must be so terrible for poor Inger.'

Those words did reach Inger's heart and, for a moment, relieved her suffering. For this was the first time someone had said 'poor Inger' and not added something about her sin. A little innocent child had cried for her sake and begged that she should be saved. She felt strange and would have liked to cry herself, but she could not weep, and that, too, was a torment.

As the years passed she heard little from the earth above her; she was talked about less and less. Down in hell's entrance hall nothing ever changed. But one day she did hear a sigh and someone saying, 'Inger! Inger! How you have made me suffer, but I thought you would.' That was her mother; she was dying.

Sometimes she heard her name mentioned by her old master and mistress; but they spoke kindly, especially her mistress. 'I wonder if I will ever see you again, Inger! After all, one cannot be certain where one will go.'

But Inger was pretty certain that her kind old mistress would not end where she herself was.

Time passed: long and bitter years. When Inger, finally, again heard her name, she seemed to see above her, in the darkness of the endless hall, two bright stars shining; they were two kind eyes up on earth that now were closing. So many years had gone by that the little child who once had wept so bitterly because of 'poor Inger' now was an old woman whom God had called up to Him. At that last moment when all her memories and thoughts of a long life passed through her mind, she remembered, too, that as a little child she had cried bitterly when she heard the story of Inger. In the moment before death, that which had happened so long ago was re-experienced so vividly by the old woman that she said aloud, 'Oh, my Lord, have I not, like Inger, often stepped on Your gifts, and not even been aware that I have done it? Have I not, too, felt pride within me, and yet You have not deserted me. Do not leave me now!'

As the old woman's eyes closed, the eyes of her soul opened for all that before had been hidden. Since Inger had been in her thoughts as she died, she now could see her in all her misery. At that sight, she burst into tears just as she had done as a child; in Paradise she stood weeping because of Inger. Her tears and prayers echoed in the shell of the girl who stood as a statue in the Devil's entrance hall. Inger's tortured soul was overwhelmed by this unexpected love from above: one of God's angels was crying for her. Why had this been granted her? Her tortured soul thought back on its life on earth and remembered every deed it had done. The soul trembled and wept the tears that Inger had never shed. The girl understood that her folly had been her own; and in this moment of realization she thought, 'Never can I be saved!'

No sooner had she said this thought, than a light far stronger that that of a sunbeam shone from heaven down upon her. Far faster than the sun rays melt the snowman, or the snowflake disappears when it lands on a child's warm mouth, did the statue of Inger melt and vanish. Where it had stood, a little bird flew up towards the world above.

Fear-ridden and full of shame, the bird hid in the darkest place it could find, a hole in an old crumbling wall. Its little body shivered. The bird was afraid of every living thing. It could not even chirp, for it was voiceless. It sat in the dark for a long time before it dared peek out and see the glory around it – for the world is, indeed, gloriously beautiful.

 It was night; the moon was sailing in the sky and the air

was fresh and mild. The bird could smell the fragrance of the trees and bushes. It glanced at its own feather dress and realized how lovely it was; everything in nature had been created with loving care. The bird would have liked to be able to express her thoughts in song; gladly would she have lifted her voice as high as the nightingale or the cuckoo does in spring, but she couldn't. But God, who hears the silent worm's hymn of praise, heard and understood hers, as He had David's when they only existed in the poet's heart and had not yet become words and melody.

Through the days and weeks these soundless songs grew within the little bird; although they could not be expressed in words or music, they could be asserted in deeds.

Autumn passed and winter came, and the blessed Christmas feast drew near. The farmers hung a sheaf of oats out on a pile in the yard so that the birds of the air should not go hungry on this day of Our Saviour's birth.

When the sun rose on Christmas morning, it shone on the sheaf of oats and all the twittering little birds that flew around it. At that moment the little lonesome bird that did not dare go near the others, but hid so much of the time in the little hole she had found in the old wall, uttered a single 'Peep!' A thought, an idea, had come to her! She flew from her hiding place, and her weak little peep was a whole song of joy. On earth she was just another sparrow but up in Heaven they knew who the bird was.

The winter was hard and harsh. The lakes were covered with ice, and the animals in the forest and the birds knew lean times; it was difficult to find food. The little bird flew along the highway. In the tracks made by the sleds she sometimes found a few grains of oats. At the places where the travellers had rested, she would sometimes find little pieces of bread and crumbs. She ate very little herself but called the other starving sparrows, so that they could eat. In town, she looked for the yards where a kind hand had thrown bread and grain for the hungry birds, and when she found such a place she would eat only a few grains and give all the rest away.

Through the winter, the little bird had collected and given away so many crumbs that they weighed as much as the bread that Inger had stepped on, in order not to dirty her shoes. As the last little tiny piece of bread was found and given away, the wings of the little bird grew larger and their colour changed from grey to white.

'Look! There's a sea gull flying out over the lake,' said the children as they followed the flight of the white bird
 that dived down towards the water and then swung itself

up high into the sky. The white wings glittered in the sunshine and then it was gone. 'It has flown right into the sun,' the children said.

PENGUIN 60s

are published on the occasion of Penguin's 60th anniversary

LOUISA MAY ALCOTT · *An Old-Fashioned Thanksgiving and Other Stories*
HANS CHRISTIAN ANDERSEN · *The Emperor's New Clothes*
J. M. BARRIE · *Peter Pan in Kensington Gardens*
WILLIAM BLAKE · *Songs of Innocence and Experience*
GEOFFREY CHAUCER · *The Wife of Bath and Other Canterbury Tales*
ANTON CHEKHOV · *The Black Monk* and *Peasants*
SAMUEL TAYLOR COLERIDGE · *The Rime of the Ancient Mariner*
COLETTE · *Gigi*
JOSEPH CONRAD · *Youth*
ROALD DAHL · *Lamb to the Slaughter and Other Stories*
ROBERTSON DAVIES · *A Gathering of Ghost Stories*
FYODOR DOSTOYEVSKY · *The Grand Inquisitor*
SIR ARTHUR CONAN DOYLE · *The Man with the Twisted Lip* and *The Adventure of the Devil's Foot*
RALPH WALDO EMERSON · *Nature*
OMER ENGLEBERT (TRANS.) · *The Lives of the Saints*
FANNIE FARMER · *The Original 1896 Boston Cooking-School Cook Book*
EDWARD FITZGERALD (TRANS.) · *The Rubáiyát of Omar Khayyám*
ROBERT FROST · *The Road Not Taken and Other Early Poems*
GABRIEL GARCÍA MÁRQUEZ · *Bon Voyage, Mr President and Other Stories*
NIKOLAI GOGOL · *The Overcoat* and *The Nose*
GRAHAM GREENE · *Under the Garden*
JACOB AND WILHELM GRIMM · *Grimm's Fairy Tales*
NATHANIEL HAWTHORNE · *Young Goodman Brown and Other Stories*
O. HENRY · *The Gift of the Magi and Other Stories*
WASHINGTON IRVING · *Rip Van Winkle* and *The Legend of Sleepy Hollow*
HENRY JAMES · *Daisy Miller*
V. S. VERNON JONES (TRANS.) · *Aesop's Fables*
JAMES JOYCE · *The Dead*
GARRISON KEILLOR · *Truckstop and Other Lake Wobegon Stories*

JACK KEROUAC · *San Francisco Blues*
STEPHEN KING · *Umney's Last Case*
RUDYARD KIPLING · *Baa Baa, Black Sheep* and *The Gardener*
LAO TZU · *Tao Te Ching*
D. H. LAWRENCE · *Love Among the Haystacks*
ABRAHAM LINCOLN · *The Gettysburg Address and Other Speeches*
JACK LONDON · *To Build a Fire and Other Stories*
HERMAN MELVILLE · *Bartleby* and *The Lightning-rod Man*
A. A. MILNE · *Winnie-the-Pooh and His Friends*
MICHEL DE MONTAIGNE · *Four Essays*
JOHN MORTIMER · *Rumpole and the Younger Generation*
THOMAS PAINE · *The Crisis*
DOROTHY PARKER · *Big Blonde and Other Stories*
EDGAR ALLAN POE · *The Pit and the Pendulum and Other Stories*
EDGAR ALLAN POE, AMBROSE BIERCE,
AND ROBERT LOUIS STEVENSON · *Three Tales of Horror*
FRANKLIN DELANO ROOSEVELT · *Fireside Chats*
WILLIAM SHAKESPEARE · *Sixty Sonnets*
JOHN STEINBECK · *The Chrysanthemums and Other Stories*
PETER STRAUB · *Blue Rose*
PAUL THEROUX · *The Greenest Island*
HENRY DAVID THOREAU · *Walking*
JOHN THORN · *Baseball: Our Game*
LEO TOLSTOY · *Master and Man*
MARK TWAIN · *The Notorious Jumping Frog of Calaveras County*
H. G. WELLS · *The Time Machine*
EDITH WHARTON · *Madame de Treymes*
OSCAR WILDE · *The Happy Prince and Other Stories*
The Declaration of Independence and *The Constitution of the United States*
Mother Goose
The Revelation of St. John the Divine
Teachings of Jesus